Ali Sparkes

freak of
fortune

From the author of Frozen in Time,
winner of the Blue Peter Book of the Year 2010

Also by Ali Sparkes:

The *Shapeshifter* series
Wishful Thinking
Frozen in Time
Dark Summer
Unleashed: A Life and Death Job

freak of
fortune

Ali Sparkes

LONDON·SYDNEY

Part of the **RÏVETS** series

First published in 2011
by Franklin Watts

Text © Ali Sparkes 2011
Cover design by Peter Scoulding

Franklin Watts
338 Euston Road
London NW1 3BH

Franklin Watts Australia
Level 17/207 Kent Street
Sydney, NSW 2000

A CIP catalogue record for this book
is available from the British Library.

Cover credits: Kev Hopgood (central figures), A-Digit/istockphoto (top),
ansonsaw/istockphoto (background).

ISBN: 978 1 4451 0556 7

1 3 5 7 9 10 8 6 4 2

Printed in Great Britain

Franklin Watts is a division of Hachette Children's Books,
an Hachette UK company.
www.hachette.co.uk

For Adam

Chapter 1: FLOOD

"Take off your glasses."

Rav tilted his head to one side. The rain was dripping off his nose. "Why?"

"Because I don't want to cut my hand when I punch you in the face."

Rav smirked. "Yeah, right." But Nic could tell he was rattled.

"I'm so scared," added Rav, turning away.

When he turned back, Nic was surprised to see Rav had taken off his glasses and pocketed them – and even more surprised to see him lift his fists.

Nic knew he could paste Rav all over Fortunestone Bridge if he wanted to. But the rain was now soaking through his jumper and he wanted to get somewhere dry. He was about to say "Naaa. It'd be too easy," and swagger away back to school when Rav just had to open his mouth.

"Come on! You might as well. It's a family tradition. It's why your dad lost his job, isn't it? Smacking his boss in the face."

Nic felt his restraint snap like a rubber band. He put his whole body weight into the punch. It sent Rav sprawling across the oily wet tarmac of the old road bridge. "THAT'S what you get for talking about my DAD!"

There was a roaring sound in Nic's ears. He guessed he must be *really* angry – he'd never heard that before. Nic didn't notice Rav get up from where he'd fallen until he slammed headfirst into Nic's stomach. The impact winded Nic and sent him rolling onto the gritty edge of the road, sucking in air like a landed fish. The roaring got louder. The weeping sky darkened a shade past charcoal.

Rav was above him, shaking with rage and the panic of unfamiliar violence. His black hair hung in clumps, showering drips as he nodded jerkily. "Not so good, is it? When someone hits back!"

"Get off!" shouted Nic.

"Coward!" spat Rav.

"NO! Get OFF!" screamed Nic. "We've got to RUN!"

The terror in his enemy's eyes made Rav look back over his shoulder.

He opened his mouth to join in the screaming. A second later it was full of water and his body was spinning over the side of the bridge.

Chapter 2: DROWNED

Nic felt as if he'd been hit by a train. He'd had only seconds to watch the frothing black fury of water plunging down the river valley towards them, roaring like a beast let out of hell, before it was upon them.

He'd been hurled backwards against the stone wall of the bridge and then flipped up over the top of it. The flash flood was filled with debris which battered his body as it whirled around in the freezing cold water. There had been no chance to grab a breath before he was hijacked by this freak of nature. He'd still been trying to draw one in after Rav's head-butt to his gut.

Nic dimly wondered what had become of his enemy. His mind flashed up an image of Rav aged four, playing in the sandpit in his back garden – before a voice in his head cried out, "I'M drowning. I should be having flashbacks about ME! Let's fit in some of ME before I die!" He knew that's what would happen next – there was no way he could get out of this alive. Yet something deeper inside him would not give up.

Nic abruptly surfaced in the wild foaming torrent. He dragged in half a lungful of air as a car tyre rafted past his face, closely followed by a dead sheep. He went under again. The roaring became muffled as water engulfed his ears. Then he bobbed up, snatching another breath, feeling some sharp debris graze his bare legs where his trousers had been torn off. Then something smashed into his chest and knocked the power from his body. And Nic was gone.

Rav anchored one bleeding arm around the weir post and hunched over, vomiting into the churning black water. River and silt and grit lurched out of his throat. He retched until finally he was done. Sticky stuff pasted his hair to his forehead and was running into his right eye. He knew it was blood because it felt warm. He looked across to the riverbank just a couple of metres away, but there was as much hope of reaching it as swimming the Atlantic. The water was deep and violent and still roaring like a monster. If he shifted even slightly he would be wrenched from the post and most likely have his bones smashed against a rock.

He couldn't hold on much longer. He was exhausted. Far in the distance he could make out the lights of Fortunestone against the swirling sky. Rav briefly imagined a helicopter coming to his rescue – but there was no one to save him. Everyone was huddled indoors, hiding from the storm. In fact Fortunestone had been huddling for months now, as the number of jobless people rose steadily. People said the town was finished – history.

Just today *he'd* told Nic that Fortunestone was finished – and he'd be out of there as soon as he hit 18 and could go to university. And Nic could stay and sweep the roads.

Now Nic was dead, he felt bad. Rav felt the swelling in his mouth where Nic had punched him. Where had that dig about Nic's dad come from? Nic's dad had taken them both to the seaside once. Nic's dad was alright. Well, he would be until they found his son's body, probably washed all the way to Morecambe Bay. A sack of skin and broken bones.

Rav turned his face up to the relentless rain and bawled for help. His fingers were numb. Soon they would lose their grip and he'd join his former best friend on the blackwater ride into the hereafter. But then something bumped against his elbow as it floated past – a car tyre. It stopped and turned, catching on something below the water. Rav grabbed it with both arms and pushed himself off the weir post. He began to spin through the raging water again, but this time towards a curve of the bank where an uprooted tree had grounded.

Rav prayed, his eyes closed. He kicked his legs and then felt a bump. His eyes sprang open – he'd hit the tree. His feet were in the shallows. He pulled himself across the mud using the branches and slumped onto the bank, panting with relief. Then he saw the body.

Chapter 3: CHASM

The eyes were open and glassy. Rav shuddered, realising how close he had come to sharing this fate.

The dead sheep bobbed on the far side of the tree, with some kind of material wrapped around one of its legs. Rav winced – it was a pair or Fortunestone School trousers.

Nic's trousers? Rav gulped back a sob. While he had been fighting for survival he'd been able to think about Nic's death almost without feeling it. Now the awfulness hit him as hard as the flashflood had a few minutes ago.

Rav leaned across the tree trunk and tugged the trousers off the dead sheep, sending the woolly corpse on down the slipstream. He flung them onto the ground and buried his face in his hands. "Nic," he cried, through his fingers. "I'm so sorry!"

"You will be if you even think about putting them on," came a voice behind him. Rav spun around, astonished. Nic stood a few metres away in just his shirt and underpants. Like Rav, he'd lost his shoes and socks and jumper. But he'd got back his trousers now. He put them on as Rav watched in overwhelmed silence.

"Where the hell are we?" grunted Nic, zipping up his flies. There was blood blooming darkly through his soaked shirt. "I don't know," said Rav. He pulled his glasses out of his pocket, amazed to find them still there and intact, and put them on.

"I don't recognise this place," said Nic. Rav followed his gaze. They were in a narrow valley. A few metres downstream, part of the river branched off and plummeted right through a jagged split in the rock face.

"I've never seen that," said Nic. Rav knew that Nic spent a lot of time exploring the fells, valleys and waterways. If Nic hadn't seen it before, Rav certainly hadn't.

"Come on," said Nic. Rav got up and followed, his bones stiff with cold and blood still seeping from his eyebrow.

The river offshoot plunged between craggy rocks, which offered a rough path along its edge. Nic set out across the rocks. The chasm was narrow and gloomy, but the sky had brightened a little; a shaft of daylight illuminated the way. "Wait! Where are you going?" called Rav. "We should head into town! We're both bleeding."

"This is new," said Nic, running his hand against the sharp-edged rock face. "All new. Look – no lichen or moss or… or anything. It's like…"

"Like what?" asked Rav, catching up.

"It's like it's just split open," murmured Nic.

Rav followed Nic's gaze as it swept up and down. The rock was dry and clean. Seams of white quartz glinted amid the stone. There was no plant life on it at all. Or any rain. "This way," said Nic, his voice suddenly excited. And he stepped towards the rock face – and disappeared.

Chapter 4: TRUTHS

Nic was amazed. Not just at discovering the cave, but at the light source. Something was glowing at the far end of this narrow sleeve in the rock. It led upwards slightly, more like a passage than a proper cave, but there was enough headroom to walk upright.

"Come on!" he called back over his shoulder, only to find that Rav was already right behind him, gaping around in astonishment.

"What is that?" whispered Rav. The glow from the far end of the cave passage reflected in his glasses.

"I don't know!" said Nic. "It shouldn't be here. This… this has only just opened up. I can smell it. It's new – dry rock. Nothing should be in here to make that light."

"It must be volcanic," said Rav.

"Here? No!" Nic sounded scornful. "This is limestone. Could have been sandstone… or a coal seam. There's nothing volcanic here."

"Yeah – right – like you're a professor of geology now! I wonder why you're not in the top set." Rav couldn't help the snotty note in his voice.

"I just remember this stuff," muttered Nic. "I'm not totally thick, you know."

"Whatever," said Rav. "Limestone or not, that light looks volcanic."

Nic paused and glanced from Rav to the light and back again. "Yeah," he said, moving on a little less certainly. "It does."

"We should go back." Rav's voice was tense. When Nic didn't respond, but just went on clambering across the uneven slant of the cave floor, Rav added, "Your dad will be worried."

"Leave my dad out of this," snapped Nic. "Unless you want another fist in your face."

Rav shook his head. "What's wrong with you?! We've just escaped death and you're still sulking about what I said today."

Nic spun around and glared at Rav. The weird light streamed around his fair head and shoulders. "I am NOT sulking about what you said today! I am ANGRY about what you've said for the last FOUR YEARS. Ever since you got moved up to Set One and decided I was too thick to bother with. OK? Got it?"

Rav gaped. "ME?! You think I stopped bothering with YOU? You've got to be kidding me." He thumped his fist against the dry limestone in frustration, causing his grazes to sting sharply. "What about when you stopped calling me Ravi and started calling me Speccy, eh? When I tried to talk to you in class and you laughed at me or just spat your gob-soggy paper pellets at me, with all your thuggy mates! Well?!"

"You – you just…" Nic tailed off. He remembered some of that stuff. He remembered the look of bewilderment and hurt on Rav's face. He remembered how the easy "Hi, mate" had gradually stopped happening when they passed in the school corridor. How he and his new friends had veered one way… to the playing fields and the roof of the gym, while Rav and his new friends veered to the computer club or the library.

"You turned into a bully," said Rav. "I don't know how we were ever friends."

Nic stared at Rav and noticed that the light on his ex-best friend's face had turned paler… a pallid shade of blue. In Rav's glasses he saw a shadow move.

Nic turned towards the light and gave a little yelp which betrayed his fear. There was a dark figure in the cave with them, blocking their path.

Chapter 5: STONE

"And still you bicker," sighed the figure. "Even with the stone near dead and fortune near turned forever."

Nic and Rav froze, staring. The dark figure was something like a man. He was thin and stooped over, with wild hair and a ragged beard. His eyes were pools of black ink with a tiny blue spark at the centre and his skin, taut across his bones, was covered with fine dust.

The figure wore a rough woven tunic and animal pelts were bound to his feet with strips of leather.

"Who are you?" Nic's throat was so dry with fright the words clicked in his mouth. "I keep the stone," said the figure. "And I watch the light. And with it the turn of your fortune. Come." The man moved back down the passage, his words pulling Nic and Rav after him.

Around a bend in the rock, the source of the pallid blue light sat at the dark man's feet. A large misshapen lump of glass or crystal – the size of a rugby ball. It had beautiful spiral markings across it. The stone was set into a cradle of rock and the shaft of light it sent up picked out the glitter of tiny quartz particles floating in the air.

Rav gazed down at the stone. "What is that?"

"It is the Fortune Stone," said the man. "And it ails."

"What do you mean 'it ails'? A stone can't be ill," said Nic. "Is the colour wrong? It was yellow before… Now it's turned blue. Is that bad?"

"You know it is," said the man. "For it is you who have turned it."

"What?" Rav wondered if he had been concussed in the river and was imagining things again.

"Who turned it?" asked Nic. "Him or me?"

The man let out a very long sigh. The blue light contracted and grew dimmer. "And there it is. Another blow to the light. See how you bring your people down? See how you turn fortune from you?"

Rav stared at the man, tilting his

head to one side, working things out. Then Rav took hold of Nic's fingers in a kind of handshake. "Sorry," he said. Nic gaped at him. This day could not get any weirder. "I mean it," added Rav. "I've said some horrible, narky things to you. I shouldn't have."

The light changed again. But this time it grew just a little brighter. Suddenly Nic understood.

"I'm sorry too," he said, and was surprised to find he meant it. "For laughing at you – and the gob and paper pellets. And… for hitting you in the face."

The light was tinged with violet now. Just a hint of warmth seeping back in. "This is it," said Nic, sinking to his knees. "This is actually the stone. It's Fortune's Stone."

The man nodded and also knelt down.

"What are you on about?" asked Rav, stooping down too.

"The ancient settlement of Fortunestone – it began with the discovery of a stone which brought good fortune to the people," said Nic, a smile emerging across his battered and bloodied face. "It was kept safely hidden and was said to be lucky – just as long as the people of Fortunestone were good to each other and lived in harmony. This… this is it?"

Rav reached out and briefly touched the stone. A frosty tingle passed through his fingers. "This is it," confirmed the dusty old man. "Dying. And so dies all the good fortune for Fortunestone."

"Can we help it?" asked Rav.

"Help it?" the blue sparks in the inky wells of the man's eyes seemed to flicker. "It is YOU who kills it."

"Why? What have we done?!" Nic spluttered. "We're just… kids. You can't hold us responsible!"

"You – Nicholas – are of the bloodline of the farmer who first discovered this stone," snapped the man. "Through you, Ravi, flows the blood of that farmer's most trusted friend. You come from generations of worthy people. But you have squandered your worth."

Rav shrugged beside Nic. "You kind of have, mate," he said.

"I think he means both of us, Rav," muttered Nic, and Rav shut up.

The man settled onto the cave floor, looking dried-up and ancient. "It is your fault. The love lost between you two has drained light and warmth from this stone for four years. It is nearly spent. And when it is gone, no good fortune will flow from it again. Your town will continue to fold in upon itself and all will die." There was a very long silence.

"So…" said Rav at length. "Is there anything we can do?"

"Yes," said Nic and for the first time

in months… maybe years… he looked right through Rav's glasses and into his eyes. "We can change. We can get back to how we used to be."

"It's too late," said the man and now he looked like a bag of dry bones on the floor. They realised the stone had dimmed again as he rested his stick-like fingers on its surface.

"No!" Rav and Nic yelled, each pressing a hand to the stone, willing something – anything – to make it glow again.

A funnel of cold air blasted out of the Fortune's Stone, knocking the old man away and making Rav and Nic shout with fear. Their hair blew up behind them as if they were in free fall and an aching, icy pain shot through their hands, up their arms and across their chests. Rav felt as though his heart was freezing. Glancing across, he could see that Nic's face was a mask of suffering, like his. "Don't... let... go!" Rav gasped, pushing his free hand down on top of Nic's. Nic shook his head.

"I won't," he grunted back, and pressed his other hand over Rav's. He thought of his dad and his father before him, and the one before that and the one before that... all struggling together to make Fortunestone a success – a safe place for their families. He pushed those thoughts down through his arms and into the rock.

Rav thought of his mother's family

line, brave and bold and fighting off marauders in centuries past. Even his father, who had married into it, was proud of his son's heritage. Could he hold on? Could he and Nic make Fortunestone survive? The cold was so intense now that it felt like their hands were frozen to an iceberg. And their whole bodies began to shiver, as if their blood was transfusing into the stone.

Suddenly there was a blast of crimson light and Rav and Nic were both flung backwards onto the cave floor, dazed and silent. In the centre of their right palm each had a livid red tattoo. A single spiral etched into the skin. The stone was glowing blood red. The light was rich and steady.

Chapter 6: TURN

knew how to play cricket. Rav got Nic

The flash flood marked the end of months of wet weather in the Lake District. As the sun returned, tourism in Fortunestone picked up and money began to flow back into the struggling shops, hotels and cafés. The nearby quarry reopened; Nic's dad got a job there. There was a new energy about the town.

Nic and Rav returned to their lives, but people noticed the change in them. They put it down to the trauma of surviving the flood. Nic was found on the gym roof less often and Rav didn't spend every break in the library. Nic taught Rav to at least look as if he knew how to play cricket. Rav got Nic into some graphic novels.

They told no-one about what they'd seen; what they had restored. As the town sprang to life around them, they guessed they'd done it right. They had gone back to look for the chasm that led to the Fortune's Stone, but it had closed up, taking the stone and its dusty guardian with it. Now fortune was in the palm of their hands. The spiral scars were a constant reminder of their link to the stone and their bond together. When Nic or Rav argued, or if either of them was in danger, the spirals tingled with a cold burn. And they never, ever faded.

About the author

Ali Sparkes is the author of the bestselling *Shapeshifter* and *Unleashed* series, and the Blue Peter Award-winning *Frozen In Time*. She's always been fascinated by the power of nature and paranormal activity. And chocolate fudge. She tried to get all three of these things into *Freak of Fortune*… but the fudge just got too wet. It had to go…

To find out more about Ali's fast-paced paranormal, action and comedy adventure stories go to:

www.alisparkes.com

JOE CRAIG
LIFTERS
From the author of the best-selling
Jimmy Coates series
EDGE

"Go! Go!" Adaq threw himself into the passenger seat. His sister, Maya, hadn't even stopped the car completely, just slowed down enough for him to jump in. She veered back out into the traffic while Adaq was still hauling the door shut.

"You get it?" she asked.

Adaq didn't respond. Of course he'd got it.

"Anyone see you?"

Adaq forced out a laugh. He managed to sound calm while he wiped his hand across his face to hide the shaking.

"How much?" Maya asked. She was always so focused on the money. "How much?" She had one hand on the wheel, the other held out to Adaq.

"Wait," said Adaq. "Give me a chance and I'll—"

As he opened the wallet his mouth stopped working: he'd never seen so much cash. Maya glanced across and for a second she went as quiet as her brother. The growl of the traffic around them sounded like the city cheering their triumph.

"Oh-my-god," Maya gasped. She jerked the wheel, cutting across two lanes, and slammed on the brakes to pull up under a railway bridge. Cars screamed past them, horns blaring.

Adaq flicked his fingers through the

coloured notes. Most were twenties, but there were fifties in there too. Lots of them. The numbers in his head soon couldn't keep up. His breath was short and his mind suddenly fogged up.

Next to him, his sister whooped and slapped the steering wheel.

"This is a good day!" she laughed.

Adaq wanted to laugh too, but nothing came out. Where was his flood of happiness? There must have been a thousand pounds in his hands. Even after he split it with Maya he'd still be the richest 13-year-old he knew. But he couldn't smile. A dead weight was pulling his stomach downwards.

"We can't keep this," he said, finally, forcing the words out between breaths.

"What?" Maya wasn't sure she'd heard him right. "Someone did see you? I knew it!" she said sharply.

"No. Nobody saw me. But..."

Adaq's head throbbed and he wanted to be sick. I can't do this any more, he thought. He shoved the money back into the soft leather wallet.

"What are you doing?" Maya said, grabbing at his hands.

Want to find out what happens to Adaq and Maya? Get hold of a copy of Lifters today!

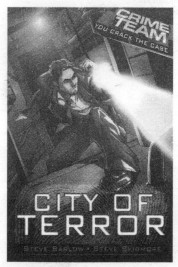
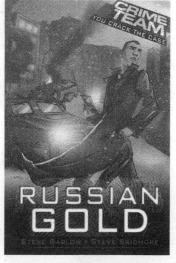